Two of  a Kind

To Alyson and Sydney, my two of a kinds
—J. R.

To Dick and Polly
—M. P.

Atheneum Books for Young Readers
An imprint of Simon & Schuster Children's Publishing Division
1230 Avenue of the Americas
New York, New York 10020
Text copyright © 2009 by Jacqui Robbins
Illustrations copyright © 2009 by Matt Phelan
All rights reserved, including the right of reproduction in whole or in part in any form.
Book design by Sonia Chaghatzbanian
The text for this book is set in Nofret.
The illustrations for this book are rendered in watercolors.
Manufactured in China
First Edition
2 4 6 8 10 9 7 5 3 1
Library of Congress Cataloging-in-Publication Data
Robbins, Jacqui.
Two of a kind / Jacqui Robbins ; illustrated by Matt Phelan. — 1st ed.
p.   cm.
Summary: When Anna abandons her best friend, Julisa, to spend time with Kayla and Melanie,
whose friendship is considered very special, she soon learns
that she has little in common with her new friends.
ISBN: 978-1-4169-2437-1
[1. Best friends–Fiction. 2. Friendship–Fiction. 3. Popularity–Fiction.
4. Individuality–Fiction. 5. Schools–Fiction.]
I. Phelan, Matt, ill. II. Title.
PZ7.R53265Two 2009
[E]–dc22 2006033210

Two of a Kind

Jacqui Robbins

Matt Phelan

Atheneum Books for Young Readers
New York ∗∗ **London** ∗∗ **Toronto** ∗∗ **Sydney**

Kayla and Melanie are two of a kind. That's what Kayla and Melanie say. Even our teacher, Ms. Becky, says it sometimes, like when Kayla and Melanie beg to be partners at work time.

Julisa and I like to be partners too, but nobody calls us two of a kind. Ms. Becky does say, "Julisa, Anna, can you help?" a lot. And we do.

At recess Kayla and Melanie sit on the jungle
gym. They pretend to do each other's hair. They
whisper and giggle.

Nobody is invited up.

At recess Julisa and I sit under the slide.
We pretend to stand up and hit our heads.

We laugh until our glasses fall off.

Anybody is invited, but nobody
comes except Henry and Matthew.

One day in science Ms. Becky says we are going to do experiments. She asks who knows what an experiment is. Julisa and I raise our hands. Julisa says an experiment is when you try something to see what happens.

When Julisa says that, I notice Kayla and Melanie laugh. Melanie holds her fingers in circles in front of her eyes like glasses. Kayla makes a face.

I put down my hand.

Ms. Becky says our experiments will be about how colors mix together to make other colors. We have to use markers and water and coffee filters. While Ms. Becky chooses our partners, Kayla and Melanie hold hands and whisper, "Two of a kind!"

I don't look at Julisa.

Ms. Becky makes me partners with Melanie.

Melanie sighs and puts her head on the desk. She says she hates science. She says why do Julisa and I raise our hands so much. She says I have to do all the work. I tell Melanie I can make a rainbow.

Melanie says the markers stink like feet.
But she takes her head off the desk.

I know just what to do because Julisa and I read all about colors at her house.

I take a black marker and draw a circle in the middle of the coffee filter.

I fill the circle all the way in with the marker.

Then I dip my pinky finger in the water and carefully let one drop fall on the circle.

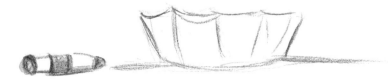

Right away the circle spreads, and I
can see all the colors that make the
marker black. Blue and green lines
squiggle to the sides of the filter.

I drip another drop and pink and
orange fill the center.

"Whoa! Anna!" Melanie yells.
Ms. Becky shushes us.

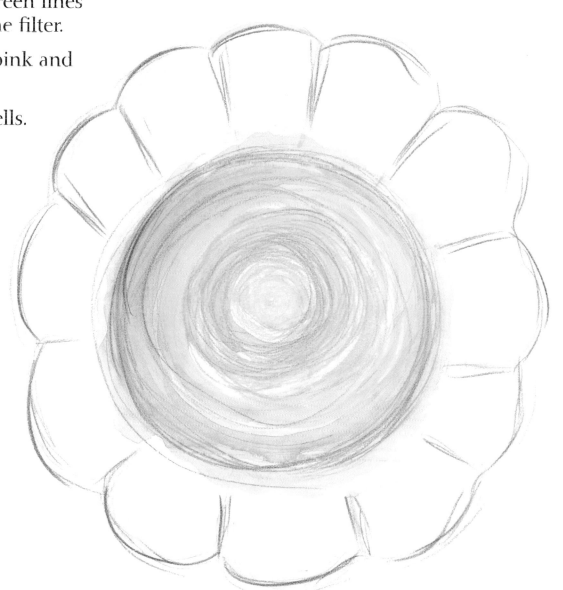

Melanie says I am so smart. She says maybe I am cool after all. She wants a turn. I let her try. She lets Kayla try. They do not drip carefully. Our cup spills. Water goes everywhere.

Ms. Becky uses her angry voice. She says we have to clean up before we go to recess.

I sigh, but Melanie touches my hair.

"Hey," she says, pulling my arm away from the mess. "Do you want to play with us?"

We do not clean up.

At recess I sit on the jungle gym with Kayla and Melanie. They pretend to do my hair. They say I should get braids. They say I should get better glasses. Melanie says, "At least she's not Miss Giant Eyes!"

Kayla laughs and points to the slide,
but I don't even have to look.
I already know who they mean.

The next day at free reading time, Julisa asks if I want to sit with her and read our favorite poem book. Kayla and Melanie ask if I want to sit on the rug. They all stare at me. I don't say a word, but I go to the rug.

Kayla and Melanie do not read. They whisper and giggle.

I peek over the top of my book at Julisa. She is sitting alone with the poem book.

Her eyes stare at it, but she never turns a page.

At lunch I ask Julisa if she read our favorite poem, but Julisa just walks away.

My stomach hurts. I can't eat anything. Kayla and Melanie take my cookies. They say, "Mmm, yum!" and dance like the girl on TV.

I remember one time I went over to Julisa's house and her dad showed us how to fancy dance. We stood on his feet and he twirled us around and around.

I look across the lunch table to Julisa. She is not eating either.

At recess I sit on the jungle gym. Kayla and Melanie pretend to do each other's hair. I watch the slide. Julisa and Henry and Matthew are laughing. Kayla and Melanie say I should get braids. They say I should get better glasses.

I would like Kayla
and Melanie to just
be quiet.

When Ms. Becky rings the bell for the end of recess,
Kayla says, "Let's stay here. Let's make someone
come and get us."

Everyone runs to the line. We do not move.
Ms. Becky calls my name and waves.

Melanie says, "Stay!"

Julisa stands below the jungle gym. She
says, "Recess is over, you know."

Kayla makes a face and laughs.
Melanie says, "We're not coming."

Julisa looks at Melanie. Her eyes are
sharp and her voice is calm. "I'm not
talking to you. I don't care about you."
And I can tell she really doesn't.

Julisa turns back to me. She blinks. "Anna?"
Her voice is shakier, like maybe now she does care.

"If you get down . . . ," Melanie says.

But I am already down. I grab Julisa's hand and run for the line.

"You're just like her after all, aren't you?" Melanie yells.

"Of course I am," I call over
 my shoulder.
"We're two of a kind."

And Julisa and I laugh until our glasses fall off.